D1491035

Whispers in the wind

Deanna Dewey

Published by

TF Film Productions Ltd

www.deannadewey.com

Copyright © Deanna Dewey
2020

ISBN   978-0-9576941-0-1

FREE Animation Download

As a **Thank You** for reading this book. There is an option for a
FREE download to my 5 minute animation film for children of Monty Mouse a story about a mouse who has no friends.

Read the book to learn about the characters and then just answer 3 questions.

Go to the end of the book to find the questions and how to obtain the free download.

Contents

Chapter 1

Meeting at Forest Farm

Secrets are strange things. They scab over like a nasty cut on the knee. But then someone will pick at an itch and the secret begins to ooze.

D al knew he shouldn't be there. They had told him often enough.

"Don't go near Forest Farm. It's dangerous, not the place for you."

Dal hid in the bushes. Spying on the girl as she cleaned out the chicken coop.

He sniffed at the air, something was not right: Everything appeared to be fine. A field of cows, pigs in their pens and chickens were scratching at the earth.

But there was no sound.

Usually there would be the moo of a cow, an oink from a pig or a chuckle from a hen.

Nothing.

The silence was strange. The sort of quiet which covers you in goose-bumps.

Dal knew something was wrong, very wrong.

He needed to get away. Dal jumped from the bushes, tripping over a bramble on his way.

The noise attracted the girl, who rushed over to him.

"Are you okay," she asked.

Dal didn't understand her. He didn't speak Hu-Mean.

He blurted out a load of naughty words in Squirrel. It was alright - she wouldn't understand him. But she did. In fact, she spoke Squirrel better than he did.

It was one of his worst animal languages so he swapped to Weaseleze. But she knew that too.

"Hu-Mean's can't speak animal," Dal snapped.

"I think you mean human. I don't think I'm a mean"

she smiled. "And I didn't know I could speak animal. I just knew what you said."

The bramble still held Dal firmly around the leg so together they very carefully untangled him. But the thorns had left their mark.

"You'd better come to the house," said the girl, "that's a nasty scratch."

Dal stared at this strange girl. She was about the same age as him.

Her freshly washed hair was fair and as long as his own dark rag tails.

It was the end of spring since Dal last washed his hair. And that was only because he fell into Hunters Pond when fishing for his tea. He remembered his wet tunic squelched and squeaked all the way back to his hide. There were only stale berries to eat that night and his wet hair and gurgling tummy had kept him awake all night.

She tugged at his arm and almost in a dream he let himself be led toward the house.

"My name's Whisper," she told him.

The name was picked up by the breeze and rustled through the long grass. It was lifted up into the air where it danced in and out of the trees.

"Whisper, whisper," the wind seemed to call.

Nearby there stood an old knarled and knobbly Mulberry tree. As the broad lush green leaves rustled in the breeze Dal thought he glimpsed a flash of something red. The leaves settled and he peered into the tree.

There was nothing there.

The sudden silence made Dal wary.

There was something strange about this place, something very strange.

For the whole ten years of his life they had warned him about this place. But why?

"What's the matter?" asked Whisper.

"I'll wait here," Dal mumbled at the back door

as he tried to peer in the window.

Whisper went into the kitchen, busying herself finding the antiseptic spray.

"Where are your mother and father?" Whisper asked.

"I haven't got parents," Dal explained. "I stay with the forest animals."

"You're so lucky. I've never seen forest animals," she was wistful. "Well only in picture books."

Dal didn't know what a book was, but wasn't going to ask.

"It's not so good," He carried on. "When I'm with the weasels they ask me where the best rabbit warrens are. When I'm with the rabbits they want to know how to avoid the weasels."

She laughed. "It must be very difficult, trying to keep everyone happy."

"They think I know where the next hunting area is."

"And you don't?"

He looked away.

"The Old Ones decide the fate of the animals."

"That doesn't seem right," Whisper was horrified.

"It's the way of the forest," Dal glanced around to check there were not any animals listening nearby. "They know to stay quiet - or it might be them on the hunting list."

Whisper had tears in her eyes.

"But how do I understand what you are saying?"

They had been talking in Weaseleze again but she had never even seen the animals, let alone learnt their language.

Surely it wasn't normal for a human girl to speak animal? And why did Dal live with animals - he should have a human family of his own.

Dal tried her on Badger, Pony, Mouse and all three dialects of Deer. She knew them all. It had taken him ten years of hard work and to Whisper it came as easy as breathing. It wasn't fair. Dal was at a loss to understand.

"Perhaps your parents taught you."

Whisper shook her head.

"Dad's away a lot - working," she replied.

"Your mother then?" suggested Dal.

Whisper smiled.

"Mum only talks to herself."

Dal looked toward the grazing animals.

"Do you talk to the oinkers and mooers?" he asked.

In Dal's world farm animals were not important enough to have names, so were only known by the noises they made.

"I've never heard them talk," Whisper said, puzzled.

"Surely, it can't always be this quiet?" Dal asked.

Whisper shrugged.

"We'll ask them," Dal turned towards the animals.

As the cows saw Dal approaching they moved away. Dal didn't speak Mooer. But he knew pony from the New Forest ponies and called a greeting. This frightened the cows and they trotted away to a far corner.

Dal was embarrassed. He hurried over to the pigs who were snuffling around for tasty morsels.

Pigs were released into the forest every autumn to eat the fallen acorns.

Dal knew a smattering of oink - so he oinked a greeting.

A couple of pigs raised their heads before quickly turning their backs.

Whisper, sensing Dal's embarrassment, walked back towards the house.

A large sow with a tummy the size of a huge balloon, watched him. He oinked again.

The pig eyed him up and down and Dal could tell she was not impressed.

"So, you're the great hope of the Forest," sniffed the sow. "You don't look very important to me. Just an ordinary grubby boy. But you should know better than to goes talking animal around here."

"I don't get it," Dal said. "The oinkers in the forest talk.

"We be pigs, not oinkers," huffed the sow. "And mighty proud we are to be pigs too. I come from a long line of Hampshire Hogs. Me name is Henrietta Hog, to you."

"Sorry!" apologised Dal. "I didn't mean to upset you. But there's something different about this place."

"Of course there is - silly boy!" Henrietta wiggled her

corkscrew tail. "We're not allowed to speak. Them Old Ones have told us - if we speak it'll be the chop."

"But why?"

"Why indeed. We're not considered important to know such things. It's wrong it is. What gives them Old Ones the right to act like gods - think they're better than us."

"They make the rules," Dal pointed out.

"And what gives them the right. I tell you if I had a second with them I'd give them a piece of my mind."

As Henrietta spoke Whisper appeared with some chocolate chip cookies.

The sow quickly clammed her mouth shut. Dal oinked at the sow, who refused to answer. The pig turned to follow her friends in the field.

"She spoke, did you hear?" he asked Whisper excitedly.

Whisper shook her head.

There was something weird going on here. And Dal was determined to get to the bottom of it.

Chapter 2

Dirty Knees

D al followed Whisper back to the house. Again, he thought he saw a movement from the bushes. He kept looking behind expecting to see something.

But there was nothing there. Nothing but silence.

As Whisper opened the back-door - Dal could hear something odd. He paused.

"It's only my mother, vacuuming," said Whisper.

Dal found the humming of the machine strangely comforting.

Without thinking he walked into the house and felt right at home. The noise was coming closer.

Dal ducked under the kitchen table just as Whisper's mother came into the room. She pushed around a purple machine that sucked everything in its wake. Bits of fluff and dirt jingled, jangled and jumbled around its insides.

Dal hoped it didn't eat boys.

Whisper's mum suddenly noticed the dirty footprints on the floor. Pulling a damp cloth from a huge pocket in her apron she bent down to clean the nasty stains.

Below the kitchen table she caught sight of Dal's dirty knees.

"Flannel needed," she announced.

And from another pocket she pulled out a pretty lilac face cloth.

"It's okay, Mum - he's a friend," Whisper said gently, taking the flannel from her mother's hand.

"Dirty ..." insisted Mrs. Stride.

"It's okay I'll give it to him."

Whisper bent down and handed Dal the flannel and whispered in Squirreleze, "Just wash your knees."

Mrs. Stride saw the dirt disappear as Dal rubbed

away at the grime. She gave a sigh of contentment. All was right in her world.

Dal peered at her through the net tablecloth and thought she was the most perfect lady he had ever seen.

Over her clothes she wore a purple pinafore with huge droopy pockets brimming over with all sorts of interesting things.

Dal could smell a faint smell of lavender and thought it wonderful. Through the lace tablecloth he saw a kind face framed with dark curls.

Mrs. Stride reached out to lift the tablecloth and Whisper heard Dal's whimper of distress.

"He's a bit shy," she explained.

Mrs. Stride let go of the tablecloth and smoothed out an imaginary crease. Then switching the vacuum cleaner back on she said, "We have work to do Charlie."

She turned and went back the way she came

pushing the vacuum in front of her.

As the noise from the machine faded in the distance, Dal scrambled out from under the table

In the distance Dal could hear the sound of a patrol of hares on the move.

"I've got to go," he looked toward the door. Dal was going to be in big trouble. He needed to leave and quickly.

Whisper was very disappointed.

"But I need to know how I can understand you."

Dal knew there were a number of questions to be answered and buried secrets to be dug out and uncovered.

"I'll meet you again, tomorrow," Dal promised. "Do you know the clearing at the bottom of the Bluebell Wood?"

Whisper nodded.

"I'll be there at sunrise."

Chapter 3

Neemis Gets Nasty

"Where have you been?" bellowed the hare in a way which would make even the bravest boy tremble.

It was Neemis, Dal's guardian, with an army of hares.

"Nowhere," Dal tried hard not to shake.

"You've been to Forest Farm," Neemis accused.

"Why would I go there?" Dal asked.

Neemis circled around the boy, sniffing his feet. "I smell lavender."

"I went through some lavender bushes," lied Dal.

"Hare's don't like the smell of lavender," Neemis growled.

"But I think humans do?" suggested Dal, cheekily.

Neemis' eyes narrowed.

"No hunting for you - for a week," he snorted.

Back home at Outfield, Dal headed straight for his hide. He had always been proud of his very own self-built home.

On first inspection it looked like a fallen dead tree. But under this hid the little hut he had built from mud and twigs.

Dal's prize possessions cluttered a corner. They

were things he'd found at picnic sites: a plastic plate with a split; a chipped mug; a crumpled page from a magazine; a picture of a house with a mum, a dad and two children smiling.

Sometimes Dal wished he were a normal human boy with a mother, a father and perhaps even a sister.

Dal took out the damp flannel from Forest Farm. He sniffed the lingering smell of lavender.

Hearing the approach of Neemis, Dal quickly

rolled the flannel up inside the picture.

Neemis burst into Dal's home and sat down on his large back feet.

"I'm disappointed in you," Neemis puffed up his orange breast, "consorting with humans, after all you've been told."

"How do you know I've been with humans?" retorted Dal.

"I can smell them on you. Disgusting things humans. Their smell lingers," Neemis snarled.

"But I'm a human boy," Dal pointed out. For the first time in his life Dal realised Neemis was afraid. But of what?

"Just remember who brought you up," Neemis snapped before lopping out of the hut.

Dal uncurled the paper. Letters on the page had smudged – but it didn't matter. Dal couldn't read or write. But the damp flannel had eaten away at the happy family and their faces had completely gone.

For a long time, Dal stared at the faceless family in front of the house.

He failed to hear something scuttle across the roof. And he didn't notice two round brown eyes peering in at him through the gloom.

S.K.

Chapter 4

Return of a Legend

Dal lay awake half the night. He didn't want to be late meeting Whisper at Bluebell Wood.

Light was just beginning to break when he stepped outside. Two hares stood either side of his home. They told Dal they were looking out for Rah the black panther who had escaped from captivity. But Rah hadn't been seen in the area for a long time.

Dal knew they were watching him. How was he going to get away to meet Whisper?

Suddenly a noise broke out between a small group of trees. Branches swayed, leaves shook and a red squirrel tumbled to the ground.

Dal had never seen a red squirrel before. He'd heard legends about them but none had lived in the forest for a hundred years.

This squirrel had a withered arm but his red coat shone with pride. He jumped up onto his feet, smoothing down a few ruffled hairs.

Neemis eyes narrowed as he immediately recognised the squirrel and bounded over shouting noises even Dal didn't understand.

But to his astonishment the squirrel came back at Neemis with such anger that no translation was needed.

Neemis was gobsmacked. Flustered, he quickly sent the other hares away. Again, Dal saw fear in Neemis' eyes.

But what could the great Neemis have to fear from this tiny squirrel.

In the confusion the squirrel looked directly at Dal and winked. It was now or never.

Dal ran and ran towards Bluebell Wood, until finally, puffing and panting he arrived at the clearing. He found Whisper humming to herself sitting on a rotting elm stump. The tree leaves seemed to be rustling in time with her tune.

Sensing Dal she turned around and smiled.

Everything was suddenly very still.

"Why do you live with the animals?" Whisper asked.

Dal shrugged.

"I was born here."

"But where's your mother?" Whisper asked.

"They told me I was found - under a tree," said Dal.

"But your mother?"

"She died when I was born.

"So, you never knew her?"

Dal shook his head.

"I don't think I can go back to the hares," Dal said changing the subject.

"You could always come back to the farm," suggested Whisper.

More than anything Dal wanted to go back and see the lovely lady. But he knew Neemis would have guards posted to watch the farm. It wasn't a safe place!

Dal was just about to answer when a large stag trotted into the clearing: a mighty animal with coat of pure white and antlers which gleamed in the sunlight.

On seeing Whisper it fled.

Dal followed.

He found the stag in a small clearing, hiding behind the mighty trunk of an old oak. The whites of the mighty animal's eyes rolled with terror.

"There's nothing to be frightened of, Treon," soothed Dal.

"Is she with you?" Treon asked, poised for battle.

Dal stroked Treon's head but the stag shook off

his hand. Dal could not understand why his friend was acting so strangely.

"Really - she won't hurt you."

Treon tossed his head.

"Stay away from her. She's evil."

"Don't be silly. She's just a girl. Come and meet her - you'll see she's okay," pleaded Dal.

"That girl's evil," insisted Treon. "You are like a brother to me and I would never lie."

"I'm going to find Whisper and talk to her."

"No," warned Treon. "It's dangerous. Evil tries to make you feel safe and comfy - then it'll attack."

Dal tried to shake off his doubts.

"You're finding shadows hiding behind every tree."

But Whisper had come looking for Dal. She hurried into the clearing, her face flushed.

Treon wasn't staying around. He bolted off.

Chapter 5

Tumble Knows More
than he Tells

Dal stared at Whisper. Was Treon telling the truth and was Whisper evil? Or was Treon lying? Dal didn't know what to think.

Before Dal had time to decide, a squirrel tumbled

out of the tree. The same red squirrel who terrified Neemis.

"Hello, who are you?" asked Whisper.

The squirrel smiled a squirrelly sort of smile.

"They call me Tumble."

Dal looked at the red squirrel with suspicion.

"My name's Whisper," she looked toward Dal who stood with his arms folded.

"And that's Dal," she continued.

"I know who you both are," said Tumble impatiently. "There are things you should know."

He shook his head unsure how much he should tell them.

"What can you know?" asked Dal. "I've never seen you before today."

"Your squirreleze is awful." Tumble dramatically placed a claw over one of his tufted ears. "It hurts to hear such a wonderful language so abused."

"Please don't be horrible to Dal." Whisper looked sad.

Tumble peered at Dal.

"You couldn't leave things alone."

"What has he done?" asked Whisper.

"Met you for a start," Tumble snapped. "That's the trouble with curious youngers. It be dangerous lifting things up and disturbing what hides underneath."

Whisper shivered. "What danger?"

"The sort which creeps up like ivy and won't let go." Warned Tumble.

"Why should we listen to anything you say. I've never seen you before?"

The squirrel stared long and hard. "Well I've seen you. And you might have seen me. But you will walk around staring at those ginormous clodhoppers of yours."

Dal looked down at his feet. They didn't seem particularly big.

He wriggled his toes. But perhaps feet looked different from a squirrelly view.

"Well I've never heard of you."

Tumble pointed to Whisper. "You hadn't heard of her, either."

"Please." Whisper pleaded. "Can you stop bickering."

"Bickering!" Tumble huffed. "I'm above bickering."

"But you are not very polite." Whisper told him off. "And we don't know you," she paused. There was something faintly familiar about this squirrel.

Something she couldn't explain.

Tumble closed his eyes as if a bad memory had jumped in front of him.

"I was dreading you both meeting. Now there's going to be questions, questions, questions."

He shook his head and opened his eyes. "Then you are going to want answers."

"I can't see what we've done to make you so upset."

Dal wagged his finger at the squirrel.

Tumble was unimpressed. "Stop doing that or I'll bite your finger."

Dal placed his hand behind his back - just in case. He knew squirrels had sharp teeth.

"But why didn't you want us to meet?"

"There was no reason for you to know." Tumble sighed. "It would have been better for the Forest if you'd never met."

"But why?" Dal pushed for an answer. "What's the Forest got to do with anything?"

Tumble settled on a branch. "I live in the Magnificent Oak in the middle of the Forest. During the old time I belonged to the Great Council."

Dal shook his head in disbelief. He had met all the members of the Council and this squirrel had never been mentioned before. He had never even heard of the Magnificent Oak.

"I left the Great Council," explained Tumble. "They have too much power and control."

"And when was this?" asked Dal - not convinced.

"About the time you were born," replied Tumble. "The time everything changed. The time we'd all been waiting for."

"Waiting for what?" asked Dal completely baffled.

"There are things you should know. I thought you were both too young. It's my fault I should've told you a long time ago."

Tumble paused and put his head to one side. Listening. Something worried him.

Dal guessed some of the secrets were about to be revealed.

"You know why Whisper can understand animal?" He held his breath.

"Too many questions," said the squirrel.

"I'm too old for all this splutter."

And off he dashed towards Death Wood.

Dal heard something, too. He bent down on his knees and placed an ear on the ground.

"It's the hares. Come on - follow the squirrel."

Before he could say anything else a river of hares poured over the hill.

"Run," Dal yelled as the hares swarmed around them.

Luckily Neemis was not with them, and without their leader the hares were badly organised. They leapt forward in one great wave and promptly bumped into each other.

Hares were flying everywhere, doing cartwheels landing on their heads and tripping over each other.

It was absolute chaos. Dal and Whisper managed to jump over them.

"Run to the woods," Dal shouted to Whisper and without looking behind her she took flight.

Chapter 6

Danger in Death Wood

Hares bounded towards Dal bumping into each other on the way. In the confusion Dal managed to dive into a bush.

Dal knew he couldn't outrun the hares. His only chance was to keep hidden and trust they wouldn't find him.

Luckily, after a while they gave up the search. No hares were willing to put a paw inside the dark, gloomy wood.

Around the rim of the woods some light managed to break through. A few bushes sprouted here and there making for good cover.

Dal darted from one bush to another until he was sure all the hares had gone. He peered into the darkness of the forest and felt goose-bumps.

The tall pine trees cut out all the light and it seemed darker than night.

Nothing grew beneath the dark canopy of the trees. Pine needles lay thick upon the floor and the only life was the creepy insects and crawly beetles which scurried around picking away at the death and decay.

Dal was worried about Whisper. Surely, she was somewhere near but he dare not call out in case the hares heard him.

Dal crept to another bush, his eyes darting in all directions.

Had anyone smelt him or seen him? Was he safe?

He was about to take a risk and go in search of Whisper when he heard the slightest rustle.

He paused and stood motionless against a dark dank tree.

Fear curdled in Dal's throat as Rah, the black panther slunk into view.

Rah had escaped from a zoo many years ago.

The panther terrified all the forest animals. He didn't speak or understand them and broke all the rules on hunting. Not even Neemis would stand up to Rah.

Dal had heard that Rah was so cunning that he even outsmarted humans who had tried to hunt him down. No Forest creature knew when the black cat might target their domain and invade their homes.

Dal knew he dare not move or Rah would surely eat him alive and leave his bones for the crows.

Even Dal's knife would be no match for those sharp teeth and razor claws.

Dal knew there was no way he could outrun the cat. He wondered, not for the first time, why humans only had two legs.

Everyone knew you could run faster on four. It was a definite weakness.

Dal had often wished for four legs, plus, of course, a

tail to balance. That was really important, too. Humans were slow, weak creatures who had to rely on their wits.

This time Dal's wits seemed to have completely abandoned him. He knew he couldn't talk to the animal. And he realised the cat could follow him up a tree.

For a brief moment he thought of the advantage of a surprise attack and drew an old knife from his pouch. He kept it well sharpened on an old stone. Dal's heart pounded. He would only have one chance.

Dal crouched low behind the bush. The cat came so near that Dal could hear the rasping and wheezy breathing and even smelt its foul stinky breath.

The panther paused, one paw in the air. Dal was down wind of Rah so surely the black cat couldn't smell him?

Dal nearly dropped his knife in fright. He tensed for the attack. But the panther had heard something else. There, on the outskirts of the woods, was a hare.

The hare was too busy looking for Dal to realise the danger ahead.

Suddenly it spied the cat and leapt into the bushes.

The panther licked his lips and followed close behind.

Chapter 7

Treon's Trapped

Whisper was well and truly lost. But she didn't mind. She felt free and alive.

For the first time she watched the birds, singing as they flew from tree to tree. Magical sounds she'd never heard before. This was a place of wonders, where everything felt so perfect and right.

She called Dal's name but there was no answer. She wondered if he had found the way to Tumble's dray.

Whisper stopped and puzzled. Something wasn't right. Before she had time to think a large black panther slunk around the corner.

Rah was in bad mood. He'd missed the hare and his lunch. He took one look at the girl in front of him and threw back his head and swore in a mighty roar.

To his amazement the girl looked straight at him and said.

"That's a naughty word."

Rah nearly fell over in shock. This strange girl was speaking panther. But how?

Suddenly there was a loud shriek and then a long whine. An animal in distress! Whisper headed towards the sound. Rah followed close behind.

There was Dal's friend, Treon caught in a trap. Whisper knew such traps were set by poachers and were illegal, as well as cruel.

Rah licked his lips at the smell of the fresh blood. He tried to rush forward but Whisper placed her hand on his back.

Rah stopped and Whisper knelt down by the panther's huge head.

He wanted to bite this girl but there was something comforting about her.

Whisper patted Rah on the head. "You really should do something about your smelly breath."

She took a peppermint out of a pocket and placed it in his mouth.

"This will help - but you could try chewing something which smells nice. And bad breath makes for bad moods."

Whisper told Rah in perfect panther. "You must go now."

Rah looked toward the injured stag.

"No! It's not his time."

Whisper patted Rah again.

"Go." She insisted.

Before Rah knew what he was doing he trotted off down the way they had come. All thought of lunch completely forgotten.

Treon tried to shake himself free, but he was gripped firmly by the hoof.

"Don't struggle," Whisper called, hurrying over to the trapped animal.

Treon rolled his eyes and Whisper read the terror in them.

"I won't hurt you," she promised.

The stag stared straight at the girl. Human girls were something to fear. But she spoke his language in a kind sort of way. His senses were still on full alert but now appeared to be telling him Whisper was okay.

But how did Rah understand her? No-one in the forest could speak to the panther.

Did this make the girl evil? Treon wasn't sure.

"I've heard stories about you," Treon said.

Whisper gave a sad smile.

"You can't always believe what you hear."

"Perhaps not," Treon said gruffly, still a bit suspicious.

Whisper bent down to free the stag from the evil teeth of the trap. The mechanism was difficult to open but eventually Whisper managed to spring it and free the stag.

"I can't believe I trod on one of those things," Treon winced. "I just wasn't concentrating ... had other things on my mind."

He flexed his leg.

"You're going to be limping for a while," said

Whisper as she smoothed the stag's leg. But the bleeding wouldn't stop. Whisper looked puzzled...

The wind picked up and the trees began to move. Cobwebs swayed in the breeze.

Without thinking Whisper gathered the cobwebs and wand them around Treon's wound. Almost immediately the bleeding stopped. How did she know such things?

"It'll be fine," said Treon.

"What are you doing so far from home?"

"Dal and I got separated. He told me to follow Tumble: a red squirrel who lives in Magnificent Oak," Whisper explained. "Can you show me the way?"

Treon knew the way to the Oak but had not been there for years.

"Are you sure? We'll have to go through the darkness."

"I'm not frightened," said Whisper. "We must find Dal. I just hope he's alright."

Against his better judgement Treon led the way through Death Wood.

Together they left the bright warmth of the sun and entered the dark wood.

The tall firs blocked out all the sunlight making the wood icy cold.

Thick dried pine needles made a prickly carpet on which they trod. With their footsteps muffled they silently walked through the gloom.

They narrowly missed a large ant hill crawling with ants.

"Sorry!"

Whisper apologised as they walked past.

Treon turned his head to look back at the ant hill. The ants were all stood on their back legs, raising their antennae's in respect.

How on earth did this girl understand Ant?

Thinking about this Treon tripped and almost fell over a large tree root. His senses now alert he heard the sound of something panting.

With his antlers he quickly pinned Whisper against a

nearby tree, keeping her quiet and still.

Whisper knew she could trust Dal's friend and kept as still as a mouse.

The noise came closer then closer still. All Whisper's muscles tensed. She could feel her heart pounding and feared anything close by would hear it too.

The stag freed Whisper and gently pushed her along the path with his nose. Whisper did as she was told.

One moment the noise seemed to come from behind, the next from in front and the next from the side. Whisper could see Treon was worried and didn't know what to expect.

In front of them stood the massive trunk of an ancient fir.

It seemed different from the others: standing tall and stately. Perhaps it was one of the original seedlings not planted by humans.

As Whisper and Treon reached the trunk they heard something close by.

Whisper followed Treon and held her breath, not wanting to make a sound.

Something moved on the other side of the tree.

Chapter 8

Strange Valley

There were three loud shrieks. It was Dal. His ears had turned red with shame and everyone laughed to try and cover their embarrassment.

"Thank goodness," said Whisper. "You had us worried."

The darkness of the woods was making everyone on edge.

Treon wasn't sure if he should be leading a human boy and girl to the ancient Oak. He understood some things were best left undisturbed.

Dal still shaken, from his close encounter with Rah, kept his head bowed.

Whisper failed to notice his gloom and just stared ahead wondering what on earth was going to happen next.

All three echoed the silent grimness of the pine wood.

"This place gives me the creeps," Dal ducked under some ivy.

A small stream tumbled along over logs and stones, then another stream which seemed the same.

"We've been here before!" exclaimed Whisper.

Dal shook his head. But the stream did seem familiar.

Treon and Dal took bearings to check they were not going around in circles.

But suddenly Whisper strode out in front - as if she knew the way. Something seemed to be calling to her.

But what?

The sunlight dazzled as they broke out into the valley. Birds chirped and a babbling brook gurgled its way alongside a large solitary oak.

The sun warmed them and the sounds of life cheered them.

They could now see the streams they had crossed were actually two circles of water.

Joining together they made a perfect figure of eight.

Dal took a sip of water from the brook. Was it his imagination or did the water taste sweeter here?

He gestured the others to take a drink.

"It's yummy," he told them wiping his mouth with the back of a grubby hand.

"Let's go swimming!"

Something held Whisper back.

Something seemed to whisper "No!" But what?

Whisper shook her head ignoring the call and jumped into the water.

The water wasn't deep enough to swim but they paddled and splashed. Wet and happy friends having fun.

All thoughts of why they were there forgotten.

An hour or so later Dal lay back on the ground. Happy and contented he closed his eyes as the warmth of the sun dried him. Whisper copied while Treon stayed on guard.

Still on his feet, Treon's eyes soon began to droop. The warmth and hypnotic effect of the valley worked and Treon was soon nodding off.

No-one was awake to notice the low, heavy mist silently rolling towards them.

They didn't notice the stream trickle to a stop or day turn to darkness.

The weary travellers slept on - an unnatural deep and heavy sleep.

Chapter 9

The Sleepy Stream

D al was warm and comfortable and in the middle of a lovely dream when he felt something nibbling on his ear. He woke up.

"Ow! That hurt," Dal said and pushed the 'something' away.

It was Tumble the squirrel. And he was angry.

"Why have you come here?" he demanded.

The mist had lifted and it was halfway through the morning.

They'd been asleep for hours. Treon was now awake too. He gently nudged Whisper with his antlers, but Whisper slept on.

"What's the matter with her?" Dal wanted to know.

Tumble sighed sadly.

"You shouldn't have brought her here," he said.

"Why not?" asked Dal.

"Get her up into the tree," Tumble ordered, "then the sleepiness should go."

"Why can't we just wake her up?" asked Dal in confusion.

"It's a special sleep," explained Tumble.

Together the friends heaved Whisper's limp body

up on to a large bough of the tree.

Droplets fell from the tree and they all looked at Whisper's sleeping face.

"Look! It's working. She's waking up," cried Dal.

Sure, enough Whisper seemed to be stirring. She took a deep breath and opened her eyes wide and almost fell off the oak.

"What happened?" she asked as she looked down at the others.

"I don't understand. The last thing I remember was drinking from the stream."

"Ah yes. The water muttered Tumble mysteriously. "Things are moving too fast. She shouldn't be back to the valley. Not yet it's not time."

Dal thought he knew everything the forest had to offer, but what about this special place? He looked toward Whisper who was staring at him. He knew she was thinking the same thing too.

Dal felt jumpy. Everything seemed completely out of his control.

Chapter 10

Ambush

"Mum's going to be really worried," said Whisper as she climbed down from the tree. "I've never stayed away before."

The tree had left its mark: her jeans and T shirt were smeared with green stains. But the strangest thing was her eyes. Her pupils had nearly disappeared and her eyes had turned the same lime green as the leaves on the tree.

Dal had never seen eyes change colour like Whisper's had. He had heard that Rah's brown eyes turned red with his victim's blood but luckily, he had never seen it. He hoped he never would either.

"We'd better get you back home," said Dal turning to Tumble. "What's the quickest way out, Tumble?"

"I'll lead you to the middle of the wood," he replied, and set off bounding from tree to tree. He was so fast that they all had trouble keeping up. It wasn't long before they recognised the path.

"You can find your own way back now," said Tumble and bid them a quick goodbye. "And stay out of the way of Neemis. He's frightened of Whisper and a cornered animal is a dangerous beast."

"But you still haven't told us what's going on,"

Dal called after Tumble's retreating back.

Whatever secret Tumble knew was going to have to wait.

Treon agreed to return to the farm with Dal and Whisper. There were plans to be made.

As the travellers were deep in thought, they failed to notice the sky turning black.

Treon looked up and yelled, "Danger!"

They all stared up. The sky was full of jet-black birds circling above.

"Lookouts for Neemis," Dal whispered. "Into the woods."

They turned to flee back the way they came.

But it was too late. One of the crows had spied the group and cawed a warning to the rest.

Realising they must make a run for it, Dal called to the others to follow him.

"Back to Forest Farm" he gasped, making a break through the last of the gorse.

Whisper followed close behind.

But Treon, uncertain, held back and hid himself among the thorns.

Dal and Whisper ran through the sparse trees. The crows followed.

Their finger-like wing feathers seemed to point at the youngsters as they sped towards Forest Farm and safety.

The sky lightened a touch and Dal quickly glanced up. The crows were holding back.

"They're giving up," he shouted.

Whisper and Dal slowed down as they tried to get their breath back. Things were going to be alright.

They started down the well-used track to Forest Farm. Whisper smiled with relief.

But as they rounded the corner the smile froze on her lips.

They had walked straight into an ambush.

For there stood Neemis, a King in full command of his animal army.

Chapter 11

The Brave Stag

D on't let them get away!" barked Neemis.

Instantly, the determined hares arranged themselves in a tight circle around Dal and

Whisper. This time there seemed no escape.

Neemis shoved his way through his soldiers and stood up on his back thumpers in front of Dal.

His large brown eyes narrowed and he hissed sounds in a language which Dal did not understand.

But Whisper did. She stared straight at Neemis and answered back.

Dal didn't know what she said but whatever it was made Neemis step away in fear.

Some of Neemis' followers began murmuring amongst themselves. They had never seen their mighty leader like this before - and in front of some silly human girl.

Neemis shook and Dal was unsure whether it was from rage or fear.

A small hare was about to ask a question but one look from Neemis silenced him. The hares were back under his control.

Neemis turned to the youngsters and sneered in squirrelly.

"Take them back to Outfield," he ordered his army.

Crows circled close above their heads making sure Dal and Whisper stayed in line. One step out of place and they received a sharp peck from a large grey beak.

Then Dal caught a glimpse of white through the trees.

What was that?

No one else seemed to notice. They carried on marching.

Suddenly from behind there was an almighty crash as Treon burst through the bushes. Dal realised he must've been following.

Treon didn't stand a chance against so many creatures.

But the determined stag was confident in the power of surprise.

Bellowing loudly, Treon leapt toward the hares. They scattered out of the way of the thump and kick of his hooves.

Crows started to dive bomb, like great black arrows piercing through the sky.

Treon stood, antlers bowed - ready for attack. A wave of crows dropped. Treon tossed them aside.

The next wave of black swooped. Instantly crow feathers flew into the air.

Hares joined in the fight, worrying away at Treon's heels. Soon the stag was surrounded.

Dal leapt forward to help his friend. For a few moments it seemed they might win.

But Neemis called out for reinforcements.

It was hopeless, but Dal was determined to go down fighting.

Out of the corner of his eye he could see Neemis standing in front of Whisper.

Even through the squawking of the crows, he heard her soft words lifting in the breeze.

"Why?   She   asked Neemis in perfect Harely,

"What have I ever done to you?"

Dal was far too busy flinging off a crow to hear the reply. The crow whizzed through the air like a dart and landed head first into the ground. Its large dagger – like beak stuck firmly in the dirt.

"Sorry," said Dal in Crower as he carefully grabbed the bird around the wings and plucked him from the earth.

"Quick, grab Whisper," shouted Treon, "and run!"

Dal broke out of the circle and grabbed Whisper by the arm.

Together they ran down the hill while hares and crows completely circled the brave white stag.

Chapter 12

Henrietta Hog Has News

"Where have you been?" Mrs Stride demanded. Dal could tell from the tone of her voice that she was not amused.

"I got up this morning, and you weren't there."

She didn't know Whisper had stayed away all night. Whisper gave a sigh of relief.

"I've been with Dal," she replied.

Then she sprinted up to her bedroom to change her clothes - still green and slimy from their escapades.

"Ah! Yes," said Mrs. Stride. "The boy who likes to sit under the table," she smiled.

"Come with me," she said.

Dal was worried about Treon. Now that Whisper was safe, he wanted to return to his friend.

But Mrs. Stride took Dal by the arm and led him to the kitchen.

Happy to watch Dal sat at the kitchen table while Mrs. Stride busied herself.

Out came a bowl, some eggs and milk from the fridge.

The only thing Dal recognised were the eggs. He presumed they came from the chickens in the farm. Dal's tummy started to growl with hunger.

Mrs Stride smiled at Dal as she cracked the eggs then mixed them together with the milk.

Dal almost forgot all the problems as he watched the kind lady. She made him feel safe.

The eggs were soon cooked and Mrs. Stride neatly placed spoonful's on slices of what Dal knew was bread. But this bread was different. It was brown and crisp from toasting.

Mrs. Stride placed a plateful of the steaming scrummy smelling eggs in front of Dal. He spooned in a huge mouthful and started cramming it down.

He would just eat this then search for Treon. He knew from experience he could hunt better if he wasn't hungry.

By the time Dal jumped to his feet Whisper had joined him, freshly showered and wearing clean jeans.

"We've got to go, Mum," she explained. And they rushed outside.

"I've got to feed the chickens," Whisper said. "Do you want to help?"

Dal shook his head.

"I'm worried about Treon," he murmured.

So, they agreed to meet up later and went their separate ways.

"I haven't got time to stop for a chat," Dal told Henrietta Hog as she waddled towards him. He was anxious to find Treon to make sure he was safe.

"I'm only trying to help," sniffed the pig. "Think you're better than you are. That's the trouble with people."

"I've got a lot on my mind," Dal tried to explain.

"I've got news," said Henrietta, "but if you're not interested ..."

Dal stopped suddenly. Secrets and suspicions were lurking under every stone. But at least the pig wanted to talk to him.

Henrietta looked around, checking to make sure they were not overheard. But it was very difficult for a hog the size of Henrietta to talk softly. Each grunt and snort echoed through the farmyard.

It only took a couple of swishes and shakes of the hog's corkscrew tail before all the animals were having their say.

The cluckers voiced their opinions by squawking and clucking. The mooers mooed their thoughts. And the baby oinkers squealed for attention.

For years all the animals had stayed silent. But no more. They made the most of sounds which had only been whispered in the dark.

Now they yelled out all at once. So, no sense could be made of what they were trying to say.

Placing his hands over his ears Dal tried to shut out the din.

Henrietta Hog was not pleased with her farmyard friends. This was her moment. She did not want it spoiled by a lot of noisy babble.

"Quiet," she roared above the animals. "It were agreed that I'd do the talking."

None of the farmyard animals wished to receive the wrath of Henrietta Hog and they all stayed quiet.

But it was too late. The noise had attracted the attention of Whisper and she joined Dal with a puzzled expression on her face.

Dal had never seen a pink pig turn white before but Henrietta Hog did and she hurried away as fast as her little trotters could take her.

The animal was clearly terrified of Whisper. But this time Dal wasn't going to let her go. He was determined she was going to tell him the truth. Even if he had to threaten to have pork chops for his tea.

Dal realised Neemis' spies probably heard the animals talking. It wouldn't be long before the farm would be surrounded. Dal turned to Whisper.

"We might have to run for it," he said.

Chapter 13

Tumble Tells The Secret

D al and Whisper were at a loss as to what to do. Even the reassuring smell wafting from nearby lavender bushes failed to lift Dal's spirits.

There was a sudden rustle then a crash as

Tumble leapt out from a nearby tree.

"Where did you spring from?" asked Whisper.

"I've had to keep my head down," said Tumble. "Spies everywhere, you know."

"We know that," said Dal crossly.

He told the squirrel all that had happened to them since last they met.

"And we were ambushed," Dal still could not believe it.

"I even tried talking to Neemis," said Whisper.

Tumble rubbed his chin.

"Interesting, mmm.. very, interesting," he muttered

"But what are we going to do?" Dal asked. "Neemis is bound to find us eventually. All the forest animals are working for him."

Dal thought for a moment.

"Perhaps if I go, Whisper will be safe."

"No! That won't make any difference," said Tumble. "Whisper is the key to everything."

"To what?" Dal urged.

Treon burst through the bushes. Battle scarred but

he stood proud and true. He glared straight at Tumble.

"It seems to me things only started going wrong when we got to know you," Treon accused.

Dal was pleased to see his old friend but he urged Tumble to carry on.

"You were there. She was here. Things had settled down..." Tumble paused.

"But sooner or later, I should have guessed this was bound to happen."

"What was bound to happen?" Whisper prompted.

"Do you know your birthday?" Tumble asked Dal.

Dal didn't know the actual day.

"Neemis told me I had seen ten winters."

"I was there when you were both born," Tumble told them.

"We were born together," said Whisper. She was very excited.

Tumble shook his head.

"Born on the same day. But in different parts of the forest."

"I was born here," Whisper replied.

"No, Whisper. You were born under Magnificent Oak."

Whisper looked puzzled.

"But Mum always told me I was born here. In the barn."

She screwed up her face, remembering what she had been told.

"Dad was away and Mum tripped and fell. No-one else was here."

An expression of sadness crossed Treon's face. So far Dal had stayed silent. His mind was working fast and furiously.

"And what about me? Where exactly was I born?" he asked.

Tumble said in a soft voice, "You were born here."

Dal's mind swished and swirled as he tried to get his thoughts around what he was being told.

"You mean," Dal couldn't quite bring himself to say the words.

"Yes," the squirrel said. "You belong here. Mrs. Stride is your real mother."

Treon took a step backwards in amazement.

Whisper was really confused.

"So, does that make Dal my brother? Am I his sister?" she asked.

"No. I'm afraid not."

The squirrel was very apprehensive.

"You don't belong here. You are the child of the forest."

Tumble went on to explain how signs in the forest had foretold of a special birth which would bring animals and human boys and girls closer together.

"Neemis convinced the Old Ones it mustn't happen," he said. "He scared them by saying that a human could end up controlling us all - forcing us to change our ways. Humans are interested in something called 'money' and Neemis told us they'd destroy our land to get at this money stuff."

Tumble gave a deep sigh as he continued. "I tried to make them see sense. But Neemis can be very persuasive."

"Not all humans are bad," Whisper interrupted.

"Even I had my doubts," admitted Tumble. "It was me who found Whisper asleep at the foot of Magnificent Oak."

"Just lying there?" questioned Dal.

Tumble nodded.

"She looked so innocent. But I knew I had to inform the Old Ones."

"You could have stayed quiet," Whisper muttered.

"Yes, I could have," retorted Tumble. "And later,

I wished a thousand times I had. Neemis wanted to kill the child."

Whisper gave a sharp intake of breath.

Did that make Tumble a traitor? Dal didn't know whether he would ever forgive the squirrel.

"But I convinced the Old Ones," Tumble continued, "I suggested we swap the baby for an ordinary human child."

Dal winced at that but nodded at the squirrel to continue.

"Well I had to do something," said Tumble. "The animals were expecting a special birth. I told them a normal child could be taught animal ways but it would never pose a serious threat."

"So, I was never more than some sort of pet," Dal said angrily.

"Never!" insisted Treon. "You'll always be my best friend."

Tumble ignored the outburst.

"I knew Mrs. Stride was expecting a baby. But it was Neemis who caused her to slip and fall in the barn.

She hit her head and went a bit doo-lally when Dal was born. The babies were exchanged and Dal taken to live in the forest."

"No wonder Mum went a bit odd," Whisper said sadly. "Although I can't even call her Mum anymore."

Tumble was apologetic.

"What was I supposed to do? You would have been killed."

Tears welled up in Whisper's eyes.

"Perhaps it would have been for the best."

"No!" Dal shouted.

But before he could say any more, the sky blackened above. A squadron of crows flew overhead completely blotting out the sun.

Chapter 14

Battle at the Farm

"To the barn," shouted Dal. He looked around for weapons. There were some old garden tools - not much use there.

A rusty knife which might come in handy, a few ancient tins of paint which could be thrown and an old vacuum cleaner.

Then came a rumbling noise. Dal opened the barn door, just a crack.

The sound was hundreds of feet, paws and claws.

There were hundreds of hares, rabbits, crows, badgers and all manner of animals following Neemis.

Treon stood his ground in the yard.

"Stop!" ordered Treon. "You don't know what you're doing."

"Oh yes I do. It's too late for talk," bayed Neemis. "Attack!"

Some of the animals waited - unsure what to do.

They didn't like the look of Treon's sharp antlers and thundering hooves. But the baying of the hare went to their head and they were soon ready for a fight.

Then Mrs. Stride appeared. She had heard all the commotion and came to see what the noise was.

She peered at the animals, not at the least bit shocked to see so many creatures invade her farmyard.

Noticing Neemis, her eyes narrowed. She now knew her nightmare had been real.

"You tried to kill my baby," she breathed, anger growing in her voice.

Then picking up one of the tins of paint she hurled it straight at the hare.

The tin opened mid-flight. Paint flew in all directions covering Neemis with streaks of yellow.

"You're not coming in here again," Mrs. Stride promised, her voice thick with vengeance.

Dal gathered up more tins of paint and Whisper joined him. Paint splattered everywhere: purple, yellow, white and blue.

Covered with paint the animals soon resembled something from a brightly coloured baby's toy box.

With paint in their eyes they couldn't see where they were going. Hares bumped into each other, but they still advanced.

"Come on Beta, you're needed," cried Mrs. Stride and grabbed hold of her old vacuum cleaner. She plugged it in and flicked the switch.

The old cleaner glugged into life. It had no suck. Instead it blew.

Mrs. Stride pointed the hose outside. It blew so hard that a crow tumbled across the yard. A hare was stopped mid bound. Another did a backward flip.

It was mayhem. Paws, hooves and claws, slipped and slid on the yard, sticky from so many tins of paint. Yellow and blue tins crashed and mingled into a yucky shade of green.

The animals slowed to a stop, trying to blink paint from their eyes.

Amid the carnage, Neemis tried to sneak away.

He knew they were beaten and he wasn't going to hang around to be humiliated any more.

But the farm animals spotted him. They looked at each other. What should they do?

But Henrietta Hog knew exactly what to do. She strolled over to Neemis

with her head held high
and promptly sat on him.

Splat!

The weight of the hefty
hog winded the hare.
Neemis had lost all dignity.
He lay there well and truly
squashed.

"You win," he gasped for breath.

"It's over. Let him go," said Whisper.

Henrietta gave a snort of displeasure but heaved herself off the hare. The once mighty Neemis crept off before anyone changed their mind.

Treon trotted over to Dal.

"Come with me," Treon urged.

Dal shook his head. Treon bowed his mighty antlers in salute before backing away with respect. Dal sadly watched him go. He didn't know what to do. He didn't know what to say.

He looked at Whisper. Somehow being the special one didn't seem so special any more.

Dal, Whisper and Mrs. Stride stood silently in the yard. Dal's feet were covered in congealing paint.

Staring down at them he wished things could be different. He tried to swallow the large lump in his throat.

Whisper bit her lip. Neither felt they had the right to be there. Neither knew what to say or do. Where did they belong?

Mrs. Stride stepped forward. A small tear trickled down her cheek. She smiled a watery smile.

"You are both my children," she sobbed, and gathered Dal and Whisper into the comfort of her open arms.

The End

FREE download

Just send me the answers to the questions about Whispers in the Wind on the next page to receive your free download to a lovely five minute children's animation film of Monty Mouse.

A complete story about a mouse who has no friends.

1. What is the name of Dal's stag friend?
2. What is the name of the squirrel?
3. What is the name of the hare?

Please go to my website
www.deannadewey.com

Then go to the contact me page.

Send me your answers and I will send you a free link.

Deanna also wrote and directed a children's feature film 'Skullz' - available on Amazon Prime

13 year old Scott Collins has a bizarre psychic connection with a glowing crystal skull. This takes him to a creepy house, even creepier occupants, a bungling criminal, a devious old lady – and a high stakes chase for his life!

Acknowledgements

The very first thanks must go to my friend, the late, Mike Plumbley, who helped with the layout and design.

Many people helped in the creation of this book and encouraged me on the way.

My heartfelt thanks to. -
Anne Marie Walker, Gemma Wilks
Elizabeth Arnold, Lexley George,
Sophie Kinsella, Jeannie Walker,
Ian & Christine Hallett, Joe Cawley,
John Bruce and Terry Wookey.

Also, to the great writers at the Blue Room Writer's group in Southampton who helped with never ending support and encouragement.

This book was finally finished with their help. Many thanks to.
Evelyn Harris, Jenni Jacombs,
Ann Victoria Roberts,
Donna Mcghie, Tessa Warburg,
Mike Hayward, Donna Mcghie,
Meraid Griffin, Mary Ann Toop,

There were so many people who helped me on this journey and apologises for anyone I may have unintendedly missed.

And of course, I must mention the wonderful New Forest, Hampshire, England, where this story is set, which gave me the inspiration for a whole series of stories and adventures with Whisper and Dal.

I hope you have enjoyed this book and please contact me if you would like to learn more about Dal and Whisper and the animals.

www.deannadewey.com

Made in the USA
Middletown, DE
05 December 2020

26323819R00093